Thank you for your support! ♡

Stacy + Sid

www.nogenderlines.com

To our beautiful little Ally,

Your beautiful and brave authentic self has
taught us more about love and acceptance
than we could ever learn in a lifetime.

We promise you Ally, to do whatever we
can to educate the world, one little soul at a time.

- So blessed to be your Mom and Dad

Well, that's a silly thing to say!

The world is full of pretty colors. Take a look around!
There's purple, orange, pink, and green, so many to be found

Colors are for everyone to cherish and enjoy.
There are no special colors just for girls, or just for boys!

"Toy trucks are for boys."

Well, that's a silly thing to say!

Toys are toys, there are no rules,
and only you would know,

the kind of toys you want to play with
as you learn and grow.

My sister Lucy loves her trucks.
You see it on her face!

I'm really glad she likes them too.
We drive, make sounds, and race!

"Ballet is for girls."

Well, that's a silly thing to say!

Ballet's a special kind of dance.
It's graceful and it's strong.

And everyone is free to learn.
We all can dance along!

My neighbor Tate takes ballet class
with me and my friend Rose.

We dance and laugh, have lots of fun,
while twirling on our toes!

Well, that's a silly thing to say!

All people can play basketball
and guess what, did you know?

If you're really good someday,
you just might be a pro!

My sister Rae plays basketball.
She's really, really good.

She dribbles fast and shoots the ball.
She rules the neighborhood!

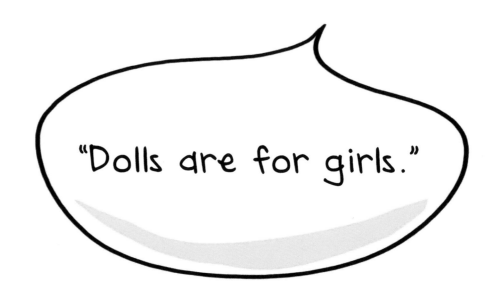

"Dolls are for girls."

Well, that's a silly thing to say!

Dolls are made to teach all children
how to love and care;

a special friend to have and hold,
to play with anywhere.

My brother likes to play with dolls.
His favorite doll is Maddy.

And when he grows up big someday,
he'll be a perfect Daddy!

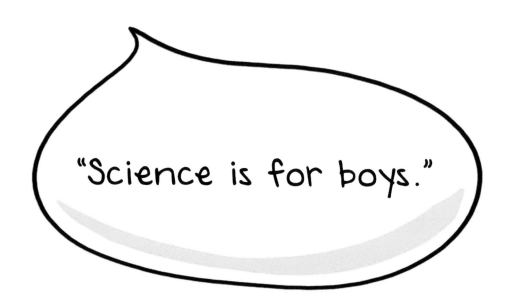

"Science is for boys."

Well, that's a silly thing to say!

Science is for everyone
to try and to explore.

Just think, you may discover things
you've never seen before!

Sadie loves experiments; they bubble, fizz and pop.
She mixes potions every day and never wants to stop!

"Gymnastics is for girls."

Well, that's a silly thing to say!

I know a boy named Jacob
who's been tumbling since age two.

He's now a star Olympian.
His biggest dream came true!

"Sewing is for girls."

Well, that's a silly thing to say!

Anyone who wants to sew
can learn to if they please.

It takes some practice, but it's fun,
and soon you'll sew with ease!

My Uncle Dan is famous.
He designs such pretty clothes.

The movie stars look stunning
in his dresses when they pose!

Well, that's a silly thing to say!

Clothes are clothes and what you wear
is really no big deal.

It's more important that you like
your clothes and how they feel.

So choose a style that you like
and pick a color too.

Be comfortable in what you wear,
the choice is up to you!

Now, that's a BRILLIANT thing to say!

When you can truly be yourself
you're happiest and free.

You get to like the things you like,
and choose just how to be.

But don't forget that others want
to be their true selves too.

So be accepting and be kind.
It's what we all should do!

CPSIA information can be obtained
at www.ICGtesting.com
Printed in the USA
LVIC04n2012161116
513254LV00004B/4

* 9 7 8 0 6 9 2 4 8 3 9 9 2 *